DISNEY · PIXAR

W9-BCA-039

Spirit *of* Adventure

A STEPPING STONE BOOK™

Random House 🏠 New York

Library of Congress Control Number: 2008934622

ISBN: 978-0-7364-2578-0 (trade)
ISBN: 978-0-7364-8068-0 (lib. bdg.)

www.randomhouse.com/kids

Printed in the United States of America

10 9 8 7 6 5 4 3 2

Spirit of Adventure

By Irene Trimble

Illustrated by Denise Shimabukuro

Hi, everybody! My name is Russell,
Junior Wilderness Explorer, Tribe 54,
Lodge 12. Being a Wilderness Explorer
is the greatest thing in the whole world.
You get to learn lots of fun stuff and wear
a special uniform!

But the very best part is the badges.
A Wilderness Explorer wears a special
sash to show all his badges. That way,
everyone knows he has wilderness skills
and that he is a friend to all nature.

I've earned lots of Wilderness
Explorer badges. I got the Kite Flying
badge when I made my own kite! That's
also when I learned that kites are not the
best way to send a message to my mom.
Next time, I will definitely use my cell
phone if I am coming home late. I also

liked getting my Archery badge. Did you know that arrows are really sharp? Ouch! I learned a lot earning that badge!

The other cool thing about badges is that when you get enough of them, you become a *Senior* Wilderness Explorer! I was really excited when I was only one badge away from becoming a full-fledged Senior Explorer. The badge I needed was the Assisting the Elderly badge. Usually, that means helping an elderly person cross the street or clean their yard or something, but that was not how it happened to me.

This whole story started when I went to the home of an old man named Mr. Carl Fredricksen. He was living in a little house in the middle of a construction site where they were building big office buildings and stores and stuff. The whole entire neighborhood had been torn down around him! I figured he might need my assistance, so I knocked on his door. It seemed kind of quiet in there, but I knocked again. A Wilderness Explorer does not give up easily.

Finally, Mr. Fredricksen poked his head out the door. He was leaning on this cane, which had three tennis balls stuck to the bottom. He had a soda-bottle cap pinned to his lapel like a badge.

I read from my Wilderness Explorer's guidebook to be sure to say everything just right. "Good afternoon. My name is Russell, and I am a Wilderness Explorer," I read out loud. "Are you in need of any assistance today, sir?"

I was surprised when Mr. Fredricksen told me that he didn't need my help, so I identified myself again as an official Wilderness Explorer. I even gave him the official Wilderness Explorer's call.

I made a *W* sign with my hands. Then I flapped my fingers like wings. "Caw, caw!" I called. After that I made the official Explorer "bear" signal and growled, "Rarrrr!"

Finally, Mr. Fredricksen looked me straight in the eye. "You ever heard of a snipe?" he asked.

I didn't know what a snipe was, but a Wilderness Explorer loves to encounter nature in all its many forms.

"Bird," he explained to me. "Beady eyes, gobbles up my flowers. You have to clap three times to lure it in." Then he looked kind of sad and said, "If only someone could catch it."

"Me! Me!" I knew I could help him.

This was the chance I needed! It took me practically a whole entire day, but I found that snipe! I did! At least, I thought I did. The snipe had a long tail and looked more like a big mouse to me. But I cornered it under Mr. Fredricksen's porch ... and that's when things really started to happen.

All of a sudden, the house began to move from side to side—and then up! Wilderness Explorer's honor, that house was being lifted off the ground!

At first I thought it might be a huge earthquake. Then I realized that if it was, Mr. Fredricksen's house would be falling down, not going up. Using my best Wilderness Explorer skills, I decided to climb up onto the porch for safety.

The house went up really fast! I scrambled as far back as I could on the porch. Things seemed a little better there, but not a lot. That's when I used my Explorer skills to think of an alternative solution: I knocked on the door.

I don't think Mr. Fredricksen was expecting anyone at that altitude. When he finally opened the door, he screamed.

"What are you doing out here, kid?" he asked.

I told him the truth: "I found the snipe,

and I followed it under your porch, but this snipe had a long tail and looked more like a large mouse." Just then, I remembered how much I wanted to get inside the house, so I cut the story short: "Please let me in?"

"No." Mr. Fredricksen closed the door.

There I was, out on the porch of that floating house all by myself again. Luckily, Mr. Fredricksen changed his mind and opened the door again. All he said was "Oh, all right. You can come in." And, boy, did I run inside superfast!

Even a Wilderness Explorer can get scared at a time like this. If you are ever on the porch of a floating house, get inside as soon as possible.

Once inside, you will have a lot of fun. I guarantee you, Wilderness Explorer's honor! See, I had never been inside a floating house before! It was so great that I forgot all about being scared! There were big sheets billowing out the windows like sails, blowing the house through the sky.

Mr. Fredricksen had this really neat model of a jungle in his house. I think it was supposed to be South America. There were also tons of old pictures of Mr. Fredricksen with a woman. I figured she was his wife. And guess what! He wore that grape-soda cap pinned to his shirt in every single picture.

Then I turned and saw a whole bunch of strings in the fireplace. I ran over there, looked up the chimney, and saw the most amazing thing in the world: Mr. Fredricksen was using about a million colored balloons to float the house!

All the strings hung down into the fireplace, where he had tied them with really good Wilderness Explorer kinds

of knots. Whenever he wanted the house to come down, he'd just cut a few balloon strings, and the house would drop a little bit. I wondered if maybe he had been a Wilderness Explorer in the olden days.

He even had this really cool atlas that was much better than the map I used when I got my Finding Direction badge. The atlas was open, and there was a drawing of a house on top of it, with the words PARADISE FALLS: A LAND LOST IN TIME.

"Are you going to South America, Mr. Fredricksen?" I asked.

"You know, most people take a plane," I said to Mr. Fredricksen, "but you're really smart because you'll have your TV and clocks and stuff!"

Then I saw that Mr. Fredricksen had also figured out a way to steer the house. He had tied a rope to a coffee grinder that turned a weather vane on the roof!

I bet he could have earned some extra-credit merit badges for that!

"Whoa!" I said. "Is this how you steer your house? Does it really work?"

I pretended I was an airplane pilot, and I turned the grinder. The whole house tipped back and forth!

"Oh, this way makes it go right, and this way's left," I said. It was fun!

I tried to get a feel for the steering,

but I accidentally tipped the house a bit too much, I think. Mr. Fredricksen kind of stumbled around.

"Kid!" he yelled kind of loud. "Would you knock it off?"

And then—oh, boy!—I looked out the front window. "Hey! We're in the city my dad works in!" It was so incredible to see everything from up in the air! "There's his building," I said.

Right after that is when I noticed something in the sky that might mean trouble. Big trouble.

I tried to tell Mr. Fredricksen politely, like a good Explorer, "I know that cloud. It's a cumulonimbus. Did you know that the cumulonimbus is formed when warm air goes by cool air?"

I tried to tell him more about it, but I think Mr. Fredricksen was still a little bit dizzy from the house tipping. He just said, "That's nice, kid," without even looking up.

I wasn't sure what to do next because I think Mr. Fredricksen wanted "quiet time"—just like what my mom wants sometimes. All I could do was keep my eye on the sky until it got really bad. That's when I had to tell him.

"Mr. Fredricksen?" I finally said. "There's a big storm coming." He still didn't look up. "Uh, it's starting to get really scary. I think we're in big trouble, Mr. Fredricksen!"

A huge lightning bolt flashed outside. And then the storm hit.

I heard this really big CRASH!—and then lots of noises that sounded like BANG! I think I even heard myself scream a little. All these things were falling down, and the house kept tipping back and forth. It was all dark inside, and then suddenly, the whole place would light up with a flash of lightning and then—KABOOM!

Wow! That was a really, really big cumulonimbus! Have you ever been inside a giant cumulonimbus cloud in a flying house before? As a Wilderness Explorer, I highly advise trying to avoid it no matter what.

I knew I had to do something, so I pulled out my electronic mapping device. I needed to move us away from the storm and toward South America!

After a while, it calmed down a little bit, and I looked at Mr. Fredricksen. He looked like he might be resting, but it didn't seem like a good kind of resting. So I started poking him in the head. It took him a while, but he finally woke up.

"Whew!" I said to him. "I thought you were dead."

"Huh? What happened?" he asked.

I was pretty proud to tell him, "I steered us! I did! I steered the house."

He rushed to the window. The house was floating on a big fogbank. "I can't tell where we are," he said.

"Oh, we're in South America, all right," I said as I showed him my Wilderness Explorer electronic mapping device. But I got really excited and I kind of waved it in the air a little too hard. It flew right out the window.

"Oops," I said.

Mr. Fredricksen and I watched as it disappeared down into the fog.

Mr. Fredricksen went straight to the fireplace and started cutting balloon strings right away. He was trying to lower the house! I think maybe he was kind of scared, and maybe a little angry.

"We'll get you down and find a bus stop," he said. "You just tell the man you want to go home to your mother."

"Whoa! It's gonna be like a billion transfers to get back to my house," I said. I had never taken a bus all the way from South America before.

We walked out onto the porch. "Here," he said, "I'll give you some change for the bus fare."

The fog was still pretty thick. "How much longer?" I asked, wondering when we were going to land.

Mr. Fredricksen scratched his head.

"Well, we're pretty high up. Could take hours to get down." That's when I looked over the edge of the porch.

BAM! I guess we were closer to the ground than Mr. Fredricksen thought. We crashed so hard that Mr. Fredricksen and I fell off the porch! For a second, I thought, *Phew! We're on land!* And then I thought, *Oh, no! There's a bouncing house right over us!* And then I heard Mr. Fredricksen gasp really loud.

It took a second before we figured out that the house was going to just keep moving. It was blowing away! Then Mr. Fredricksen made a kind of grunting noise, and he actually started running a little bit, chasing the house.

"No!" he yelled. "My house! Wait!"

A green garden hose was dragging behind the house, and Mr. Fredricksen made a leap for it. I didn't think he could jump like that, but he did. He grabbed the hose and—WHOOSH!—just like that, he was pulled up into the air!

"No! No! Wait!" he kept telling the house.

I knew right then and there that Mr. Fredricksen needed the help of a true Wilderness Explorer. I ran and grabbed his foot before it was too high to reach.

"Russell, hang on!" Mr. Fredricksen yelled down to me. We skidded toward the edge of the big cliff. We were going to fall right off! When I looked down, I saw a canyon that was about a zillion miles deep!

Oh, boy! Did I ever try to dig my feet into the ground! Mr. Fredricksen screamed, and so did I!

Then, right at the edge, we stopped.

"Walk back!" Mr. Fredricksen yelled down to me. "Walk back!"

At first, I didn't want to move! Then I gave it a try. I yanked really, really hard on the garden hose. It worked! I guess I'm stronger than I thought I was. The house was moving away from the cliff!

Mr. Fredricksen was still hanging from the hose. He squinted his eyes. There was still a lot of fog.

"Where are we?" he asked.

Then the fog cleared. You will not believe what we saw then. . . .

"There it is!" Mr. Fredricksen shouted. "Paradise Falls!"

It was the most amazing place in the whole world! There was so much jungle around, I thought we might see a T. rex or something.

"Ellie," he said, looking at the falls, "it's so beautiful!" I didn't ask any questions just then, but I was pretty sure that Ellie was that lady with him in the old pictures. And I got the feeling that she wasn't around to answer him anymore. He just talked to her.

"We made it! We made it, Russell!" Mr. Fredricksen said. Paradise Falls was only a few miles away. "We could float right over there! Climb up!"

I was going to get to assist Mr. Fredricksen again! I scrambled to grab the hose and began to climb.

"When you get up to the porch," Mr. Fredricksen grunted, "go ahead and hoist me up!"

I tried and I tried. But still I could only get a few inches above his head. And then I just ran out of strength and slid down on top of his head.

"I'm not that good at climbing," I admitted. Most of the other Wilderness Explorers did it pretty well, but I couldn't.

But then I got another idea. "We could walk your house to the falls!"

"Walk it?" he asked me

I told him, "We weigh it down. We could walk it right over there like a parade balloon!"

Mr. Fredricksen looked over at the falls. He didn't seem too sure at first. But then he seemed to really like the idea.

Using my Wilderness Explorer skills, I tied sheepshank knots in the hose to make harnesses. Now we really could pull the house!

That's when Mr. Fredricksen told me the rules: "We're gonna walk to the falls quickly and quietly, with no rap music or flashdancing."

I didn't really know what he meant, but that was okay. I just couldn't wait to get started!

"We have three days, at best, before the helium leaks out of those balloons," he told me. That's when he took out that drawing that had been lying on top of the atlas. It was the drawing of the house, and the house in the picture was right on top of those exact same falls where Mr. Fredricksen wanted to take his house!

"Don't you worry, Ellie," he said. "We'll get our house over there." Then he started walking.

"Uh, Mr. Fredricksen, if we ⎯
get separated, use the Wilderness
Explorer's call." I showed him how ⎯
make the wings with my fingers, and
then I did a really loud birdcall. "This is
fun already, isn't it, Mr. Fredricksen?
Don't you worry, I'm gonna assist you
every step of the way!"

Mr. Fredricksen seemed to be really
listening to me a lot, because he only
interrupted about one time. "Hey," he
said. "Let's play a game. It's called *Who
Can Be Quiet the Longest*."

It was so cool! My mom loves that
game, too! So we played it for a little
while. And we walked and walked and
walked. Everything was really quiet,
except for sometimes when a jungle
noise made Mr. Fredricksen's hearing
aid go off.

"Darn thing!" he yelled. I understood

why he seemed kind of grumpy. I was feeling tired and hungry and really hot and thirsty by then, too.

"C'mon, Russell," Mr. Fredricksen said. "Would you hurry it up?"

But I couldn't help it. My knees hurt. My elbows hurt, too. "And I have to go to the bathroom," I told him.

Mr. Fredricksen rolled his eyes. "I asked you about that five minutes ago!"

"Well, I didn't have to go then," I said.

Mr. Fredricksen could see I wasn't really walking anymore. I was letting the house just kind of pull me along. Finally, I plopped down in the dirt. "Can we stop now?" I asked him.

"Russell! If you don't hurry up, the tigers will eat you!"

I told him there are no tigers in South America. I knew this because I have a Zoology badge.

Mr. Fredricksen closed his eyes tight. "Oh, for the love of Pete! Go on into the bushes and just do your business."

I remembered my Privacy and Cleanliness training from Wilderness Explorer camp, and I was so excited to try it! I took a little shovel out of my pack and went behind some bushes. But I forgot one part.

"Mr. Fredricksen? Am I supposed to dig the hole before or after?"

Then I remembered. "Oh, it's before!" I yelled. Mr. Fredricksen didn't answer. He just made a kind of groan. Anyway, while I was still back there, I spotted something on the ground . . . animal tracks! They were all around.

There was no match for this footprint in my Wilderness Explorer's guidebook. It could only be one thing. *Whoa!* I thought. *Snipe.*

I looked at the tracks really close.

"Here, snipe," I called out, clapping my hands. "Come on out, snipe!"

I followed the footprints until they stopped. I knew it must be close by.

I decided to take out a chocolate bar and think it over. That's when I heard something rustling in the bushes behind me. I turned around. Nothing was there.

Then, from behind me, something leaned over my shoulder and took a bite out of my chocolate! This time I turned around really fast. "Gotcha!" I yelled. I saw the thing duck into a bush.

I peeked my head through the branches and did my best to lure him out. "Don't be afraid, little snipe. I am a Wilderness Explorer, so I am a friend to all nature." I held up my chocolate bar just out of his reach. "Want some more?"

It worked! An orange beak came out

of the bushes and nibbled on my chocolate bar. I backed up a little so the snipe would have to come out to get it. And that worked, too! But I was a little surprised when he stood up.

He looked kind of like a bird, but he was taller than Mr. Fredricksen. Way taller. He was really colorful, too. I'd never seen anything like him before. He was probably the most awesome thing I had ever seen, ever!

I got the snipe to follow me back to Mr. Fredricksen. "I got a snipe," I told him.

"Oh, did you, now?" he said. I guess he had seen lots of snipes before, because he didn't seem too excited.

I wanted to make sure I really had found a snipe. So I just asked him, "Mr. Fredricksen, are they tall? Do they have lots of colors? Do they eat chocolate?"

That's when he looked up. He saw the bird and screamed, "Aiigh! What is that thing?" Mr. Fredricksen pulled me away from the bird and shouted, "Go on! Get out of here!" He poked his cane at the big bird. "Go on!"

The bird hissed.

"No, no, no, no, no, Kevin," I said. "Mr. Fredricksen is nice." Then I patted Mr.

Fredricksen on the head so Kevin would get the idea.

"Kevin?" Mr. Fredricksen asked me.

"Yeah, that's the name I just gave him." (I'm good at making up names.) Kevin patted Mr. Fredricksen's head with his beak and I thought, *Wow! Kevin likes him, too! This is going to be great!*

But Mr. Fredricksen just yelled, "Hey! Beat it! Vamoose! Scram!"

That's when Kevin snatched Mr. Fredricksen's cane and tried to swallow it! But it was kind of lumpy and big, so Kevin spat it back out. It landed at Mr. Fredricksen's feet, tennis balls and all.

The cane looked okay to me—just a little goopy. But Mr. Fredricksen started shouting, "Shoo! Get out of here!"

But Kevin wouldn't go. That's when I asked, "Can I keep him, please?"

Mr. Fredricksen said "No!" so fast that

I could tell he didn't want to talk about it anymore. So I recited the Wilderness Explorer's motto: "An explorer is a friend to all, be it a plant or a fish or a tiny mole."

"That doesn't even rhyme," Mr. Fredricksen said.

"Yes, it does," I said.

Then Kevin got up on the roof and started pecking at the balloons!

"You come down right now!" Mr. Fredricksen yelled.

Kevin slid down the hose. I *really* wanted to keep him. He would be the coolest pet in my whole neighborhood!

I decided to ask Ellie. I thought Mr. Fredricksen might let me keep Kevin if I got her permission. So I looked up at the house and said, "Uh, hey, Ellie! Could I keep the bird? . . . Uh-huh?" I cannot tell a lie. I didn't really exactly hear Ellie, but I pretended to so that I could keep Kevin.

"She said for you to let me," I told Mr. Fredricksen.

He looked up and started talking to Ellie: "But I told him no!" Then all of a sudden, he got kind of red in the face and turned to glare at me.

"I told you no!" he said. I decided not to ask again for a little while.

I looked at Kevin. I was sad, and I did not want to leave him. Then I put my harness back on, and Mr. Fredricksen and I started pulling the house again.

As we walked along, I dropped bits of chocolate on the ground so Kevin could follow us. I didn't want to disobey Mr. Fredricksen, but I also, as a Wilderness Explorer, had promised to be a friend to all nature. And that meant giving some chocolate to Kevin so he could follow us.

Then someone yelled out from the fog, "Hey, are you okay down there?"

We looked really, really hard through the fog. Then we saw a man! I was a little bit scared, but Mr. Fredricksen walked right up to him!

Of course, being attached to Mr. Fredricksen and the house, I went, too. But when we got close, we saw that the "man" was just a big rock. In fact, there were a lot of big rocks that looked like other things.

"Whoa!" I shouted to Mr. Fredricksen. "That one looks like a turtle! Look at that one. That one looks like a dog!"

Then the "dog" rock moved. WHOA! It *was* a dog! I love dogs!

Mr. Fredricksen called into the mist, "We have your dog." But nobody answered.

The dog was so awesome. He did everything I asked him to do! No kidding! When I told him to sit, he sat. When I told him to shake, he reached out and shook my hand.

Then I told him to speak.

"Hi there," he said.

Wow! The dog could talk!

I guess Mr. Fredricksen had never heard a dog speak before, either. "Did

that dog just say 'Hi there'?" he asked.

The dog liked Mr. Fredricksen right away. "My name is Dug," he said. "I have just met you, and I love you."

Then the dog explained that he had a really amazing electronic collar. "My master is a good and a smart master. He made me this collar so I can talk." Then he turned his head fast and shouted, "Squirrel!" I think that was a dog thing. He must have really liked squirrels.

Dug's collar had lots of fun-looking buttons. I started playing with them. The buttons made Dug speak in a whole bunch of different languages.

"I would be happy if you stopped," Dug said when I switched him back to English.

"My pack sent me on a special mission," Dug said. "Have you seen a bird?" Then, all of a sudden, Kevin just leaped out of the bushes and tried to tackle Dug. "That is the bird! May I take your bird back to camp as my prisoner?" Dug begged.

"Yes! Yes!" Mr. Fredricksen shouted. "Take it!"

Dug was so cool! "May we keep him?" I asked Mr. Fredricksen.

"No," he said.

"But he's a talking dog!" I quickly pointed out.

All Mr. Fredricksen did was grumble, "It's just a weird trick or something."

I was really happy because I was keeping *both* Kevin and Dug! We were like a little parade. Mr. Fredricksen was in the lead, followed by me, followed by Kevin, who was followed by Dug, who kept saying to Kevin, "Please be my prisoner. Please be my prisoner."

That night, it rained a lot. We tied the

house to a rock. I tried to put up a tent for Mr. Fredricksen. It didn't work very well. There were a whole lot of poles!

"Tents are hard," I finally said to Mr. Fredricksen, and sat down next to him.

"Why didn't you go ask your dad how to build a tent?" he asked.

"Well, he's away a lot," I said. Then I told him how it was even pretty hard to call my dad on the phone.

Mr. Fredricksen just said, "Oh," and smiled like everything was okay. I guess it was because the house was protecting us from the rain anyway. But I also think it was because he was just being nice.

"Why don't you get some sleep?" he told me.

That's when I decided to ask Mr. Fredricksen again if we could keep Kevin. And guess what! He finally said it was all right! He even promised. I fell asleep really happy that night.

The next morning, the rain was gone. But so was Kevin!

I told Dug to find Kevin right away. I started looking, too.

"Kevin!" I shouted. "Where are you?"

Then we heard a noise up on the roof. Kevin was sitting on a pile of food he'd taken from Mr. Fredricksen's kitchen.

"Hey, get off my roof!" shouted Mr. Fredricksen.

All of a sudden, Kevin turned and made a really loud call.

"The bird is calling to her babies," Dug said.

Her babies? "You mean Kevin is a girl?" I said to Dug. I couldn't believe it! Kevin couldn't be a girl. Her name was Kevin! (But I guess that was kind of my fault, since I gave her that name.)

Just then, Kevin made another really

loud call. This time, a tiny noise from far away answered back. WHOOSH! Kevin slid down the hose really fast!

"She has been gathering food for her babies and must get back to them," Dug said. "Her house is over there in those twisty rocks." The rocks were huge and crooked. They made a giant maze. Dug told us that if she went into those rocks, she wouldn't come out for a long, long time. Then Dug would get in trouble with his master.

I was really sad when Kevin hugged me good-bye.

But as she headed home, we suddenly heard something tear through the jungle. Kevin ran and hid before she even got to the twisty rocks. You want to know why? Three of the most humongous dogs in the world leaped out at us superfast! They all wore collars like Dug's and

spoke human, too. There was a really big
Doberman named Alpha, a rottweiler
named Beta, and a huge bulldog named
Gamma. They growled and circled us.

There was something wrong with
Alpha's collar, and he spoke in this funny
high voice like a cartoon character.

Alpha squeaked at Dug, "Where's the
bird? You said you had the bird."

Dug nervously told the dogs that he'd have the bird tomorrow.

Alpha squeaked again, "Well, at least you have led us to the Small Mailman, and the One Who Smells of Prunes. . . ." Small mailman? Me? I knew I wasn't the one who smelled like prunes, because that was Mr. Fredricksen.

Then the three dogs told us they had to take us to their master.

"What?" Mr. Fredricksen looked pretty angry. "No! We're going to the falls. We're not going with you."

But those dogs started growling again and we got scared, so we went with them. After a while, we reached the opening of a gigantic cave. It was so big and humongous that we even got to bring the house inside.

The cave was dark, too. Then we all saw a bunch of glowing eyes moving closer and closer to us. It was a pack of other dogs with a really old man—older even than Mr. Fredricksen. The old man was leaning on a cane.

He looked up at Mr. Fredricksen's house. "You came in that?" he asked us. "In a house? A floating house?"

The man started laughing really hard. Mr. Fredricksen looked more closely at the man and suddenly said, "Wait! Are you Charles Muntz? *The* Charles Muntz?"

The old man frowned. "Who wants to know?" he asked.

"Jiminy Cricket! Is it really you? I'm so glad to see you alive! My wife and I were your biggest fans!" Mr. Fredricksen said. It was weird to see him so excited. It turned out that Mr. Muntz was a world-famous adventurer back when Mr. Fredricksen was a kid like me.

I think that Mr. Muntz was glad somebody remembered him. He looked pretty proud when Mr. Fredricksen told about being his fan. It was kind of nice. Mr. Muntz even invited us to go to his home with him!

Pretty soon we were pulling the house behind Mr. Muntz and his dogs on the way to Mr. Muntz's home. We walked

through a huge arch and—whoa!—there was a giant old-fashioned dirigible (kind of like those blimps that fly over the baseball games). It was floating right there inside the cave! Mr. Fredricksen's jaw dropped.

"We're not really going in the *Spirit of Adventure*?" he asked, all excited. (The *Spirit of Adventure* was the dirigible's name. I figured that out by myself.)

We tied the house to a rock and climbed up the dirigible's gangplank. All the dogs followed us—all except poor Dug. Alpha made him stay behind and wear the Cone of Shame, like the ones from the vet that dogs hate.

"I do not like the Cone of Shame," Dug said. I felt really sorry for him.

Mr. Muntz led us through the *Spirit of Adventure*. The place was like a giant museum or something.

"Jiminy Cricket!" Mr. Fredricksen said again. Mr. Muntz let Mr. Fredricksen play with everything. Then we got dinner served to us by dogs!

"Ah, my Ellie would have loved all this," Mr. Fredricksen said. He took out the picture Ellie drew of their house on Paradise Falls. "That's why I'm here," Mr. Fredricksen said with a smile. "I made her a vow."

I was really hungry, so I wasn't really paying a lot of attention to what they were saying. I was not being rude. I think I was actually being polite, allowing them to talk without interruptions. (My mom sometimes tells me that I should practice not interrupting.)

Then Mr. Muntz showed us a giant skeleton. It looked just like Kevin!

"Hey! That looks like Kevin!" I said.

"Kevin?" Mr. Muntz asked.

"My new giant bird pet!" I explained proudly. "She likes chocolate!"

And—oh, boy!—Mr. Muntz started going kind of crazy. He said that a whole bunch of people had come before us to find this rare bird. He wanted to be the one to catch it—nobody else. Now he thought *we* wanted it!

"Uh, we really should get going," Mr. Fredricksen said quickly.

But Mr. Muntz wouldn't let us leave! "You're not leaving," he said. "You haven't even had dessert yet." It sounds nice, but I don't think Mr. Muntz was being nice. I think he knew that we had Kevin and we weren't going to tell him where the bird was.

Then all of a sudden, Kevin cried out really, really loudly. It was kind of bad because now everybody knew that she was with us. But it was also kind of good because it distracted Mr. Muntz and all his dogs.

Mr. Fredricksen and I just ran down the hall, through the trophy room and down the gangplank. I think it was the best thing to do at that point.

Mr. Muntz watched us through the window. Then he looked up at the house and saw Kevin on the roof!

"LIARS!" Mr. Muntz cried. I didn't think we really had *lied* about anything. We just hadn't really talked about where Kevin was. Mr. Muntz turned to his dogs and yelled, "Take down the house!"

Mr. Fredricksen and I untied the house
as fast as we could.

"Hurry!" Mr. Fredricksen said. The
dogs were chasing us really fast!

Then all of a sudden, a great big beak
snatched me off the ground. It was Kevin!
She threw me on top of her back and
grabbed Mr. Fredricksen, too. We held
on tight as Kevin ran toward the opening
of the cave with us and the house.

We were almost there when the house
crashed into a giant rock. I fell off Kevin's
back. Kevin kept going, but the dogs
were getting really close, and I was kind
of dragging along the ground.

Suddenly, an avalanche of rocks
stopped the dogs.

It was Dug! He had made the rocks
fall and saved us!

"Go on, Master," he said to Mr. Fredricksen. "I will stop the dogs."

Good old Dug. I liked that dog! It was too bad that the other dogs knocked him over. Still, he made it outside the cave right after us.

Then I remember yelling "Help!" A lot. We were dangling over a canyon that was way too deep and much too wide to jump.

Mr. Fredricksen looked up at the house. It was still flying. Plus, the wind was moving it out ahead of us. We kept holding on to Kevin and floated with the house off the edge of the cliff.

The bad part was that Alpha nipped Kevin's leg.

Luckily, we made it to the other side, but Kevin's leg was really hurt. I used my Wilderness Explorer first-aid training to wrap it in a bandage. But when she tried to stand, her leg was just too sore. She

made a really loud call. I knew she had to get back to her babies. She needed some help.

Even though Mr. Fredricksen wanted to get his house to Paradise Falls more than anything else in the world, he finally said he would help Kevin. Good old Mr. Fredricksen! With Kevin on the porch, Mr. Fredricksen, Dug, and I pulled the house as fast as we could.

It was already pretty dark when we finally heard Kevin's babies cry. We were almost there! We tied the house to a rock and started running toward the giant maze of rocks.

Kevin limped up the hill.

"That's it, Kevin! Go find your babies!" I shouted to her. But just before she got into the maze, a big spotlight shined right on her. It was coming from Mr. Muntz's floating dirigible! Then a net shot out and trapped poor Kevin!

"Give me your knife," Mr. Fredricksen told me. He started sawing at the net.

"I wouldn't do that!" Mr. Muntz yelled.

Then he threw a kerosene lantern on Mr. Fredricksen's house, and it caught on fire! Mr. Fredricksen took one look and dropped the knife.

"No!" I screamed. With Kevin still stuck in the net, the dogs grabbed her and took her into Mr. Muntz's dirigible.

Mr. Fredricksen took off his jacket and beat out the flames around his house. I was glad that he saved his house and everything, but I was still really mad at Mr. Fredricksen.

"You gave away Kevin!" I said. I even started to cry a little bit. "You just gave her away!"

Mr. Fredricksen put on his harness and said, "Whether you assist me or not, I'm going to Paradise Falls."

He started walking again. The house was harder to drag by now, especially since Mr. Fredricksen was doing it all by himself. Still, I did not assist him. Not at all. I just walked off to the side by myself as he dragged the house and finally got to Paradise Falls.

That is when I took off my sash and threw it down hard. "I don't want this anymore," I told Mr. Fredricksen. He was already climbing the steps of his porch to go into the house. I guess he only cared about accomplishing his mission.

So I decided to rescue Kevin by myself. I took some of the balloons off the roof to help me fly back to her. It was pretty hard to hang on to the balloons, and they were running out of helium. Luckily, I had found a leaf blower. As soon as I turned it on—WHOA!—it jetted me through the air pretty fast.

Then I got my wish—but not exactly the way I had planned. I did get to the dirigible, but Mr. Muntz's dogs trapped me in maybe three seconds. They have a very good sense of smell.

After the dogs took me to Mr. Muntz, I got locked up and tied to a chair. I didn't know what was going to happen next,

but I didn't tell Mr. Muntz anything. Loyalty is very important to a Wilderness Explorer. So Mr. Muntz left and ordered the dogs to guard me.

I felt a little stuck, to tell the truth. I just sat there and tried to think of all the Wilderness Explorer skills I could use to try to get out and rescue Kevin.

You'll never—I mean never—believe what happened next.

Mr. Fredricksen found me! And just in time, too! Mr. Muntz opened the gangplank. Then he slid me and the chair down the plank. It might have been fun if I had been sledding, but I could tell that this ride was not going to end in a fun way, seeing as how we were at the edge of one of those huge crevasses again.

Anyway, good old Mr. Fredricksen caught me in the nick of time by using his water hose to pull me up to the house. I guess he had changed his mind about me, because he had flown his house to find me. He had Dug with him, too. I think Mr. Fredricksen was happy to see that I hadn't floated all the way to Bolivia. But we were still really in trouble.

"Get me out of this chair!" I yelled. I knew Kevin was still in that dirigible, and I had to save her!

But all Mr. Fredricksen said was "Russell, be quiet!" Then he jumped back onto the dirigible with Dug, leaving me behind.

They were going to save Kevin!

I hopped my chair onto the porch to get a better look. Whoops!—I hopped right off the porch and got my chair wedged between the house and the dirigible. I was looking down into the humongous canyon again.

Luckily, a Wilderness Explorer never gives up, because about a second later, the dirigible started to move away. I grabbed Mr. Fredricksen's garden hose, and then I slid superfast to the bottom of the hose. The jolt knocked the chair right out from under me. Whoa!

There I was, dangling from the house, when a whole bunch of biplanes flew out of the dirigible. Mr. Muntz's dogs were the pilots! It was so amazing! A dogfight! But it wasn't like watching a movie or

anything like that. This was real!

That's when I saw Mr. Fredricksen with Kevin. They were climbing up the ladder on the side of the dirigible. And Mr. Muntz was chasing them! Honestly, I didn't know that any of them could climb a ladder like that. I was even more amazed that Mr. Fredricksen was trying to save Kevin!

All of a sudden, I felt really strong, like I could do anything. I climbed up that hose and onto the porch!

I think I might've seen Dug in the dirigible's cockpit. That's when I got this really great idea. I remembered how much Dug loved squirrels. So I yelled, "Squirrel!" really superloudly. And then I saw all the dog pilots flying all over the place. Pretty soon they had cleared out. It was so cool!

But Mr. Muntz wasn't ready to give up. He was still climbing that ladder, chasing after Kevin and Mr. Fredricksen.

Suddenly, Mr. Fredricksen hit Mr. Muntz with his cane. It was pretty close, but Mr. Muntz still hung on to that ladder!

I knew it was my turn to help. I was the only one on the house, and I knew I could help rescue everyone with it. I grabbed the rudder and tried to steer. Mr. Fredricksen was yelling, "Russell! Over here!" I looked down and saw that Dug was with them now.

I steered the house over the top of the dirigible. Mr. Fredricksen hoisted Kevin onto the porch, then Dug. He was doing that hero thing—when the hero gets everybody else safe before he jumps on board. Well, right when Mr. Fredricksen was about to jump on board the house, one last biplane zoomed in. It popped about half of the balloons holding up the house! I knew we were in trouble then. The house just kind of slowly dropped and landed right on top of the dirigible!

Then the house started sliding over the edge of the dirigible—with Kevin, Dug, and me inside. I didn't know what was going to happen next, but it didn't look very good. Then Mr. Fredricksen grabbed the garden hose. Way to go, Mr. Fredricksen! He was trying to keep the house from sliding over the edge!

That's when Mr. Muntz came back. He even had a rifle with him. He jumped onto the porch and beat on the door! He wanted to get Kevin!

Dug and I held on to Kevin and we tried to hide.

"No!" Mr. Fredricksen yelled at Mr. Muntz. "Leave them alone!" Good old Mr. Fredricksen. He was trying to help us. All of us—including me, Dug, and even Kevin!

Mr. Muntz kicked in the door. Then Mr. Fredricksen got an idea. "Everyone hold on tight!" he yelled. "Bird!" he called, waving a chocolate bar for Kevin to see. "Chocolate!" Mr. Fredricksen remembered! He remembered that Kevin loved chocolate!

Kevin bolted out the big front window of Mr. Fredricksen's house. Dug and I were clinging on to her back. We had escaped Mr. Muntz! Sort of.

Then something really bad happened. The hose's attachment broke, and Mr. Fredricksen's house started sliding fast. It took Mr. Muntz right with it as it fell over the edge of the dirigible.

We all just stood quietly right next to Mr. Fredricksen as he watched his house fall and disappear into the clouds below.

"Sorry about your house," I said to Mr. Fredricksen. I really wished I could've done something. You can pretty much tell that someone really loves their house if they drag it all the way to South America.

"You know, it's just a house," he said. Then he looked at Dug, Kevin, and me— and he did the weirdest thing: He smiled. I never saw him do that before.

We all climbed into the cockpit of the

Spirit of Adventure. Mr. Fredricksen was so cool. He just took the controls and lowered it to the ground.

We took Kevin to the twisty rocks where her babies were waiting. The babies were so cute and fuzzy! I really, really wanted to keep one. But I knew they were Kevin's.

Even Mr. Fredricksen liked the babies. I think he even giggled when they climbed all over his head and tickled him.

Finally, I gave Kevin a big hug and climbed back into the cockpit. Kevin called out to say good-bye, and I yelled back, "Bye, Kevin!"

"Ready?" Mr. Fredricksen asked me.

"Ready!" I answered. The dirigible flew into the sky. Dug and all the other dogs stuck their heads out the windows as we soared away. That's when Mr. Fredricksen picked up my Explorer's sash and put it over my head.

When we finally got home, I was all dirty and stuff, but I still went to the Wilderness Explorers' badge ceremony. When I was about to get my Assisting the Elderly badge, the troop leader asked for my dad to come up. But, see, my dad wasn't exactly there.

Then all of a sudden, Mr. Fredricksen just stood up in the audience! He said he would give me my badge, just like a dad, only more like a granddad.

Except he didn't give me my Assisting the Elderly badge. He gave me something even better. He took the soda-bottle cap off his jacket. He had worn it all the time because it was a gift from Ellie. He pinned it to the empty space on my sash. I couldn't believe it!

"The Ellie badge! For performance above and beyond the call of duty!" Mr. Fredricksen said, and saluted me.

"Wow!" I said. It was the best badge I had ever earned!

"You and me, we're in a club now," he said.

And guess what? A whole bunch of Mr. Muntz's nice dogs, including Dug, started barking in the back of the room. It was like having my own fan club or something.

I think that was the best day of my life so far. Afterward, Mr. Fredricksen took us out for ice cream, just the way my dad used to, and we named the colors of the cars as they passed by on the street. It was really nice. And I liked it a lot when Mr. Fredricksen drove me home in his new house—the dirigible. It was pretty cool. Dug lived with him, too. And now I know that whenever I want to visit them, I just have to call, and we can go pretty much anywhere we want.

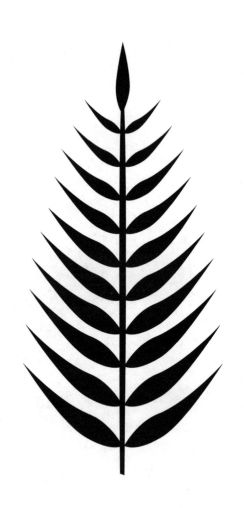